Disney THE JUNGLE Book

MOWGLI'S

RAINY DAY

PaRragon

Bath • New York • Cologne • Melbourne • Delhi
Hong Kong • Shenzhen • Singapore

WRITTEN BY BRITTANY RUBIANO

ILLUSTRATED BY MINGJUE HELEN CHEN

This edition published by Parragon Books Ltd in 2016

Parragon Books Ltd
Chartist House
15–17 Trim Street
Bath BA1 1HA, UK
www.parragon.com

Copyright © 2016 Disney Enterprises, Inc

All rights reserved. No part of this publication may be reproduced, stored in a retrieval system or transmitted, in any form or by any means, electronic, mechanical, photocopying, recording or otherwise, without the prior permission of the copyright holder.

ISBN 978-1-4748-5409-2

Printed in China

There once lived a man-cub named Mowgli.

Mowgli lived in the Jungle with the wolf-mother, Raksha, and the rest of her pack.

He had many friends from all parts of the jungle, like the leisurely turtles...

and the spirited flying squirrels ...

the chatty pangolins and porcupines...

and the honest rhinos.

But none were quite like Bagheera, the wise panther,

or Baloo,
the happy bear.

Bagheera taught Mowgli the Law of the Jungle.

FOR THE STRENGTH OF THE PACK IS THE WOLF,

AND THE STRENGTH OF THE WOLF IS THE PACK.

And **Baloo** taught **Mowgli**
to make his own path ...

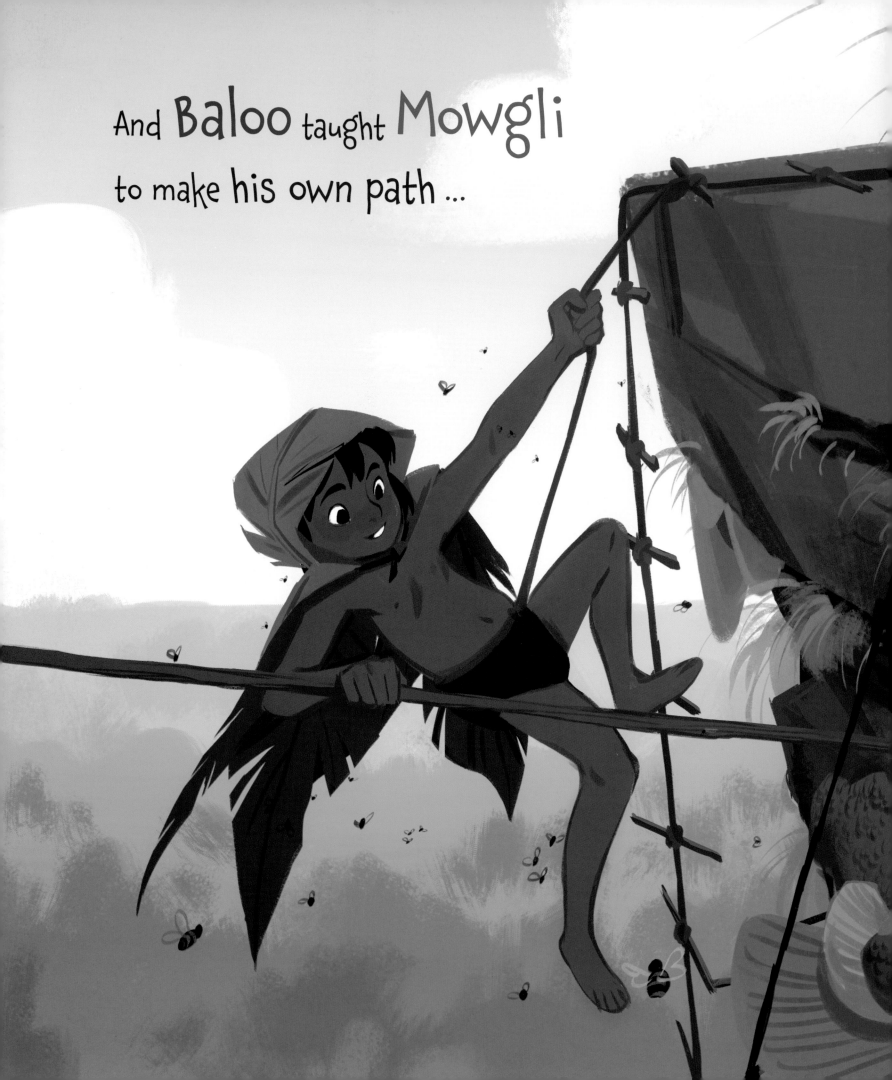

a path that sometimes
ended with **honey.**

Bagheera pointed out which plants were poisonous.

And **Baloo** pointed out the juiciest berries.

Bagheera made sure Mowgli knew
when to cover his tracks from predators...

while **Baloo** encouraged Mowgli
to relax on the river –

no track-covering necessary.

Most importantly, Bagheera taught Mowgli to respect all the creatures of the Jungle.

And **Baloo** taught **Mowgli** to **Stop** and **enjoy the view.**

One day, dark, heavy clouds swirled in the sky.

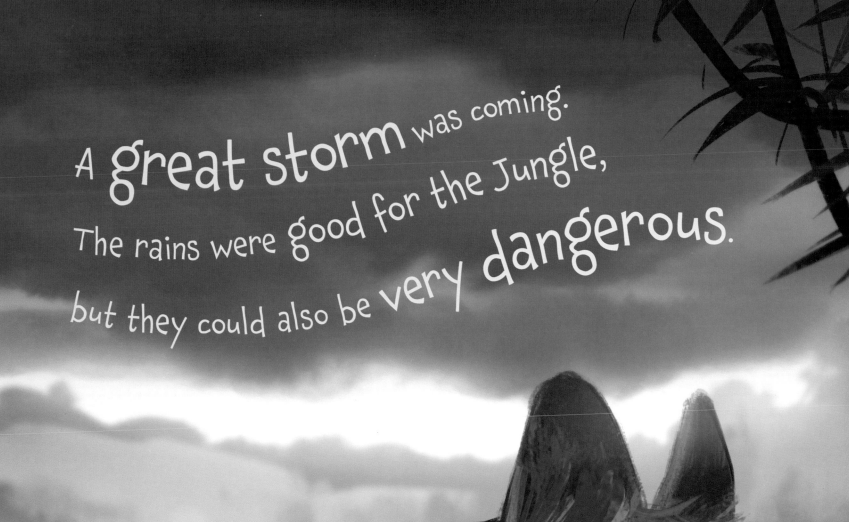

A great storm was coming. The rains were good for the Jungle, but they could also be **very dangerous.**

Bagheera told Mowgli to have something to eat and take cover. The storm would start at any moment!

While **Baloo** liked the idea of eating,
he was not worried.
Rain was **fun!**

Suddenly, it started to pour.

Bagheera took shelter in Baloo's cave.

He insisted that Mowgli and Baloo join him.

They should at least get under the thick trees, **Bagheera** told them. That much water at once was bad for the fur.

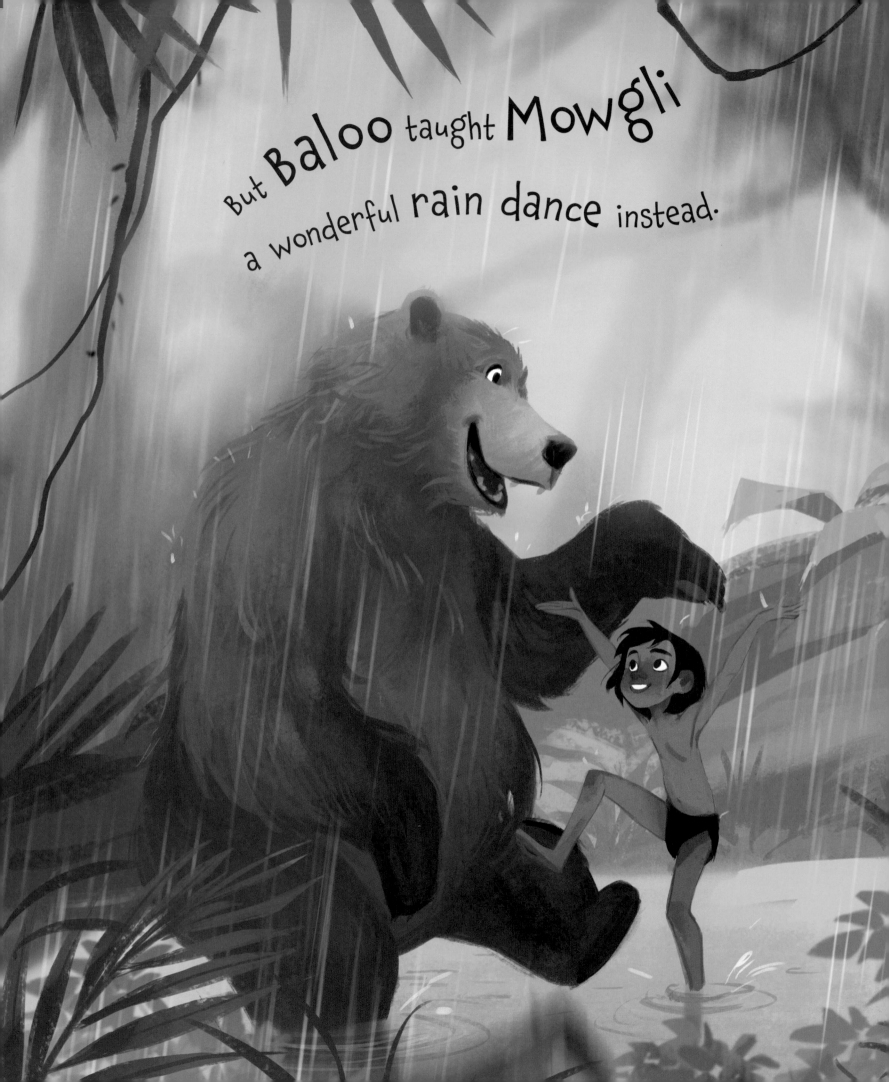

But Baloo taught Mowgli a wonderful rain dance instead.

They asked Bagheera to dance with them.

Bagheera did *not* like that idea.

Again and again they asked
Bagheera to join the fun.

But still he refused.

So the bear and the man-cub went on with their dance.

Bagheera sniffed the air. They *did* look like they were having fun. He took a step outside.

It was just as he had suspected –
Bagheera did not enjoy
rain dancing.

After a while, Mowgli felt cold and tired. He joined Bagheera in the cave.

Baloo started to feel hungry. It would be much too hard to get honey in this weather.

He joined Bagheera, too.

The cave was warm and dry.
Bagheera had even gathered
some of **Baloo's** stores of food
for them to eat.

It was **marvellous**.

Later that night, Mowgli thought about
how lucky he was to have friends
who could teach him so many things –
the bare (and *panther*) necessities of life.